Max and Jane

By Milliana Rosa
Illustrated by Nan Brooks

Target Skill *Review*
High-Frequency Words *Review*

Scott Foresman
is an imprint of
PEARSON

Jane and Max like to play.
They can play a game.

Jane came to play.
Max came to play.
They like to race.

Mom and Dad have a box.

It is a big red box.

It is a gift.

What is in the box, Mom?

You can take the box.

Jane and Max take the box.
They look in the big red box.

Look! Jane and Max see a cat.

It is Kate, the little cat.

Kate has a little tail.

Kate is little and soft.

Jane and Max like Kate.

Kate likes Jane and Max.